MONSTER HEROES

THE WEREWOLF BULLY

BY BLAKE HOENA
ILLUSTRATED BY DAVE BARDIN

STONE ARCH BOOKS
a capstone imprint

Monster Heroes is published by
Stone Arch Books, a Capstone Imprint
1710 Roe Crest Drive
North Mankato, Minnesota 56003
www.mycapstone.com

Library of Congress Cataloging-in-Publication data
is available on the Library of Congress website.
ISBN: 978-1-4965-6415-3 (library binding)
ISBN: 978-1-4965-6419-1 (paperback)
ISBN: 978-1-4965-6423-8 (eBook PDF)

Summary: A new mummy has started at school, but he's really just
a human in disguise. Brian the zombie and his friends know they need to
protect the new kid from Harriet the werewolf and her gang of bullies.
The Monster Heroes come up with a plan that makes the human boy
seem like the scariest monster of all. A glossary, discussion questions,
and writing prompts complete this early chapter book.

Book design by: Ted Williams
Photo credit: Shutterstock: Kasha_malasha,
design element, popular business, design element

Printed and bound in the United States.
PA 021

TABLE OF CONTENTS

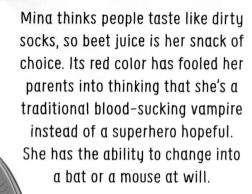

Mina thinks people taste like dirty socks, so beet juice is her snack of choice. Its red color has fooled her parents into thinking that she's a traditional blood-sucking vampire instead of a superhero hopeful. She has the ability to change into a bat or a mouse at will.

Brian is the brainy one amongst his friends. Unlike other zombies, Brian prefers tofu to brains. No matter what sort of trouble is brewing, Brian always comes up with a plan to save the day, like a true superhero.

BRIAN *(the Zombie)*

WILL *(the Ghost)*

Will is quite shy. Luckily he can turn invisible any time he wants because he is a ghost. When Will is doing good deeds, he likes to remain unseen. His invisibility helps him act brave like a real superhero.

With a wave of her wand and a poetic chant, Linda can reverse any magical curse. She hopes to use her magic to help people, just like a superhero would.

LINDA *(the Witch)*

HARRIET

BRRRIIINGGG!!!

Classes at Frankenstein Elementary were about to start. Ghouls and ghosts floated across the playground. Ogres and orcs stomped toward the front steps. Monsters of all sorts rushed through the doors.

Brian nervously watched. He took a deep breath.

"Okay, you can do this," he told himself.

Brian was smart. He liked school. No, he *loved* school. He was the student who asked for homework every night. His classmates found that super annoying.

But something on the other side of those doors scared him. And her name was Harriet Lycoan. Harriet was a werewolf. She was part person and part wolf.

In the sky above, a full moon shone. Brian glanced up at it and shivered in fear.

"Oh great," he said. "It's going to be a bad night of school."

Brian took another deep breath. Then he joined the flow of monsters entering the school. He hoped he would just blend in.

But he was not that lucky. A hairy hand grabbed Brian's shoulder. It yanked him backward.

"It's Brainy Brian!" Harriet said. "How's it going, *Foul Meat?*"

Behind Brian's hairy bully stood a werecat named Kitty and a feathery werebird named Polly. They were all half human and half animal.

"Foul Meat! Foul Meat!" Polly repeated. "Ha! Because he's a zombie."

Just as Brian was about to become lunch meat, Kitty grumbled, "Who is that?"

Through the doors walked a strange-looking mummy.

"It's a new kid," Harriet growled.

"Some *old meat*," Kitty snarled.

"Ha! Old meat! Old meat!" Polly repeated. "Because he's a mummy!"

Harriet let go of Brian. He plopped to the ground with a thump.

"We're gonna have some fun with the new kid after school," Harriet snarled.

Once the bullies walked away, Brian headed to class.

THE NEW KID

During computer lab, Brian sat next to his friend Will.

"Have you seen the new kid?" Brian asked. "He's a mummy."

"Boys can't be mommies," Will said.

Brian rolled his eyes.

"*Mummy*. Not *mommy*," he said.

Next, Brian had language arts with his friend Linda.

She was chanting a poem. "Eye of newt and toe of frog, wool of bat and tongue of dog," she said.

As Brian sat down next to her, Linda asked, "Did you memorize your chant for today? It's a really fun one."

Of course he had. Brian never skipped homework. But something else was on his mind.

"Have you seen the new kid?" he asked Linda. "He's a mummy."

"Yeah, I saw him with Mina," Linda replied.

Mina was a vampire. Like Will and Linda, she was one of Brian's best friends.

After class Brian found Mina in the cafeteria. She was sitting with the new kid. Will and Linda were also there.

Brian sat down with his friends. He looked from the new kid to Mina. Something was weird.

"Hey! Is this toilet paper?" Brian asked.

"Maybe," the new kid muttered.

"Are you a human wrapped in toilet paper?" Brian asked.

"Yeah," Mina said, blushing. "It's my neighbor Greg."

"I wanted to come to school with Mina tonight," Greg said.

"Well, now you're in serious trouble," Brian said.

Brian told his friends about the werebullies.

Most monsters thought it was funny to scare people. But not Brian and his friends. They wanted to be like superheroes. They wanted to save the day and help people.

"What are we going to do?" Will asked.

"We can't let those bullies hurt Greg," Mina said.

"Yeah, I don't want to be an after-school snack," Greg said.

"We won't let you become bully bait," Mina said.

"Mina, you gave me an idea," Brian said.

THE SUPER SUN

After their last class, the friends met by the front doors.

"Everyone know the plan?" Brian asked.

Everyone nodded.

With a *POOF!* Mina turned into a bat. Will dropped his sheet and disappeared.

Then Greg stepped out the doors. Mina and Will ducked behind him.

The three werebullies were waiting outside.

"Hey, it's chow time," Harriet snarled.

"Chow time! Chow time!" Polly repeated. "Because we're—"

"You need to stop that!" Kitty grumbled.

"It is really annoying," Harriet growled.

As the bullies argued, Will and Mina grabbed Greg's wrappings. They whirled around, pulling the wrappings off. Then they whirled around, wrapping up the bullies.

"Hey, what are you doing?" Polly squawked.

"It's just toilet paper," Kitty grumbled.

"Hey, he's just a boy," Harriet snarled at Greg. "Let's eat!"

Before the bullies could do anything, Linda burst through the doors. She waved her wand in the air and chanted, "Bullies become undone under a bright yellow sun."

And *POOF!*

Instead of nighttime, it was daytime. Instead of a full moon, the sun hung overhead.

"Oh no!" Harriet and the bullies shouted.

One by one, they went missing. *POOF! POOF! POOF!*

The werebullies were now just three kids wrapped in toilet paper.

Then was Brian's turn. He stepped out the door and held his arms in front of him.

"Brains!" he groaned. "Brains!"

He lumbered toward the bullies.

"Brains! Brains!" Polly squawked. "He's going to eat our brains!"

The bullies got up and ran away.

"Ha, if only they had half a brain," Mina said.

"They'd know Brian prefers meatballs," Will said.

Brian high-fived Linda.

"We saved the day!" he said.

"Just like real superheroes," Linda said.

DAVE BARDIN

Dave Bardin studied illustration at Cal State Fullerton while working as an art teacher. As an artist, Dave has worked on many different projects for television, books, comics, and animation. In his spare time Dave enjoys watching documentaries, listening to podcasts, traveling, and spending time with friends and family. He works out of Los Angeles, California.

BLAKE HOENA

Blake Hoena grew up in central Wisconsin, where he wrote stories about robots conquering the moon and trolls lumbering around the woods behind his parents' house. He now lives in Minnesota and continues to write about fun things like space aliens and superheroes. Blake has written more than fifty chapter books and graphic novels for children.

GLOSSARY

bait—food used as a trap for catching animals

chant—to say a phrase over and over

foul—unpleasant or disgusting

ghoul—an evil spirit

lumber—to move at a slow pace

memorize—to learn by heart

orc—a mythical creature

snarl—to growl, usually showing teeth

whirl—to move around quickly in a circle

THINK ABOUT IT

1. Bullies are scarier than monsters! What would you do if you ran into a bully?

2. If you could choose between being a vampire, a witch, a ghost, or a zombie, which would you choose to be? Why?

3. Brian and his friends don't want to scare people; they want to be like superheroes and help people. If you could be a superhero, how would you help people?

WRITE ABOUT IT

1. Write a schedule of Brian's classes. What subjects do you think they teach at Frankenstein Elementary?

2. Greg uses toilet paper to sneak into school with Mina. Now write about a day that Mina sneaks into Greg's school. What do you think might happen?

3. Write a paragraph about a time you have been "the new kid," (whether that be on a sports team, at a school, or with a group of friends). Try to use as many details as possible to capture what you were feeling.